D1286109

for NANA, *the walking woolsack:*
too odd even for this book.

Adam's Book of odd Creatures

verse and pictures by JOSEPH LOW: Atheneum / New York

. . . the Lord God formed every beast of the field, and every fowl of the air; and brought them unto Adam to see what he would call them: and whatsoever Adam called every living creature, that was the name thereof.

GENESIS II: 19

ncestor Adam thought he'd done

With naming creatures, one by one:

The moose, the mouse, the crocodile

And thousands more—it took a while.

He wiped his brow and said, "Ah, me—

I'm quite done in." But just then he

Spied some left over: twenty-six.

"Oh!" Adam cried, "A pretty fix!

SENSIBLE
NAMES

*Use these
first*

"The sensible names have all been used.

My poor brain's tired. I'm so confused.

"Was ever man so sorely tried?

I've all those letters yet, beside,

Ancestor Adam thought he'd done

With naming creatures, one by one:

The moose, the mouse, the crocodile

And thousands more—it took a while.

He wiped his brow and said, "Ah, me—

I'm quite done in." But just then he

Spied some left over: twenty-six.

"Oh!" Adam cried, "A pretty fix!

SENSIBLE
NAMES
*Use these
first*

"The sensible names have all been used.

My poor brain's tired. I'm so confused.

"Was ever man so sorely tried?

I've all those letters yet, beside,

"To place in order alphabetical;

Anything less would be heretical."

The sun dropped down; the sky grew dimmer,

And Eve, he knew, was waiting dinner.

He wept, he wailed, he cried a bucket;

He tore his hair, he screamed, "Nantucket!"

He stubbed his toe against some rocks,

Which brought to view another box.

"I think that I may say," said he,

"This is a real emergency.

"Still, if I work fast, and the creatures run,

We may finish the job and beat the sun.

"Creatures," he cried, "You, you, and you!

Pass by in line. Not two by two—

"Save that for Noah and his ark

Long after you have left this park.

"In single file will be much better,

And as you pass, each take a letter."

So, picking up a letter, he

Beckoned the first and said, "Let's see . . .

"You're to be alewife. Here's your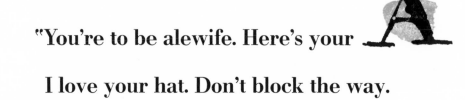

I love your hat. Don't block the way.

"**B**, basilisk; if looks can kill,

I'm bound to say I think yours will.

"Goodness, gracious, Cassowary!

Your feathers look so very hairy.

"**D** dodo is, poor passing thing;

He will not last: he cannot sing.

"Wig?" said Adam. "Earwig," said he;

"I'll take that letter there: the E.

"O, flounder, you are beastly flat;

So **F** for you, and that is that.

"G goes to gnome

who's never neat,

And yet his mother

thinks he's sweet."

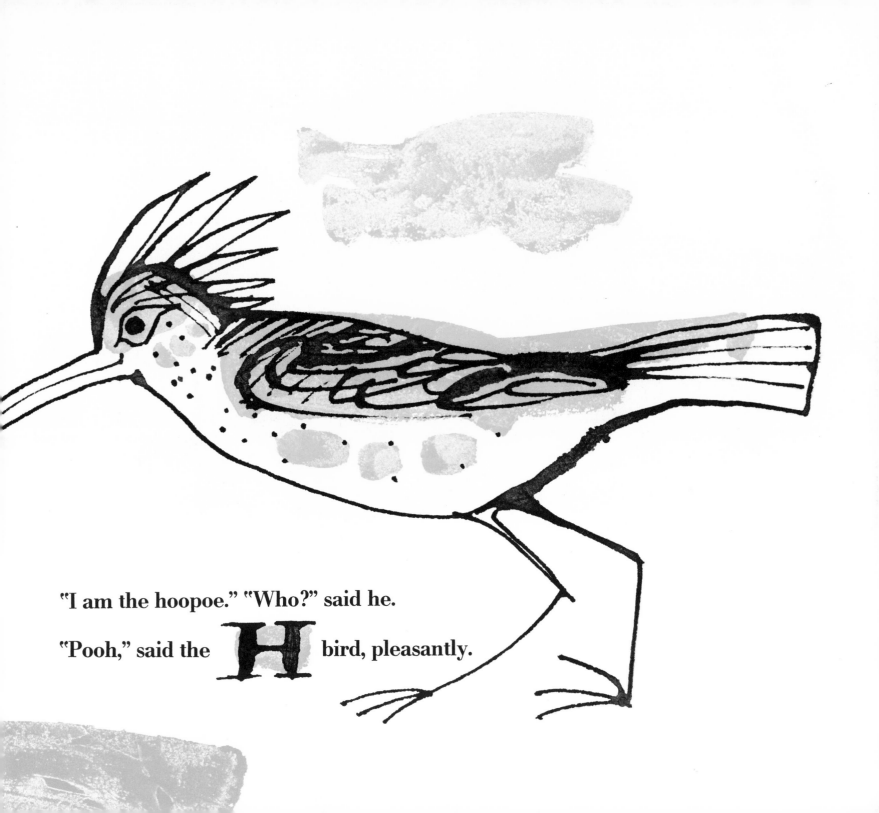

"I am the hoopoe." "Who?" said he.

"Pooh," said the **H** bird, pleasantly.

"Ug," said the Iguana, "I

Shall carry off the letter I."

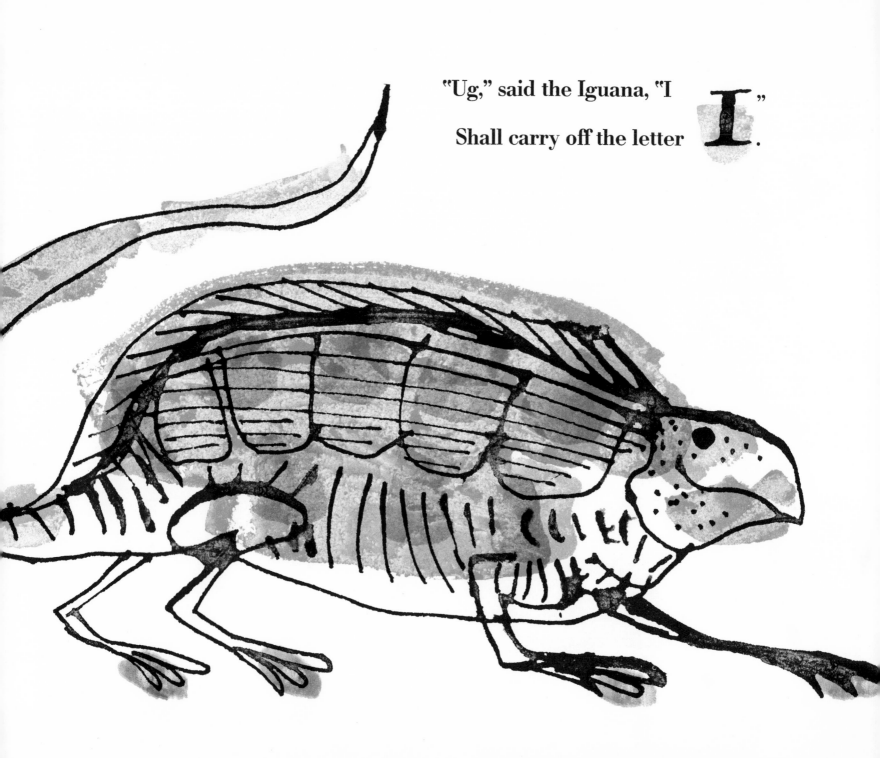

"Jumping jerboa gets the J.

What's next?" said Adam. "Can it be K?"

"Katherine, Kitty, Katydid —

What did she do? . . . She really did?

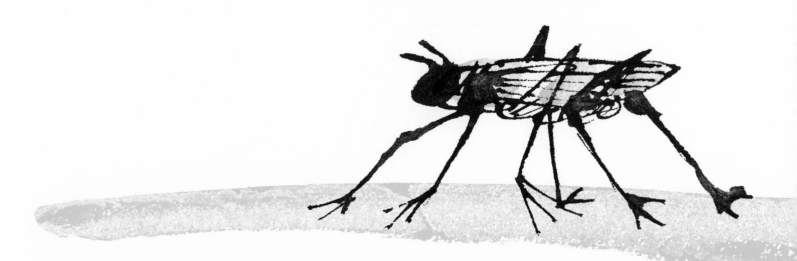

"Lovely little **L**adybug,

You must ask Eve to weave a rug.

"Mandrill, your face

is sad and long,

How shall I cheer you?

Sing a song?"

"No," said the narwhal, "Not the P—

N is the letter meant for me."

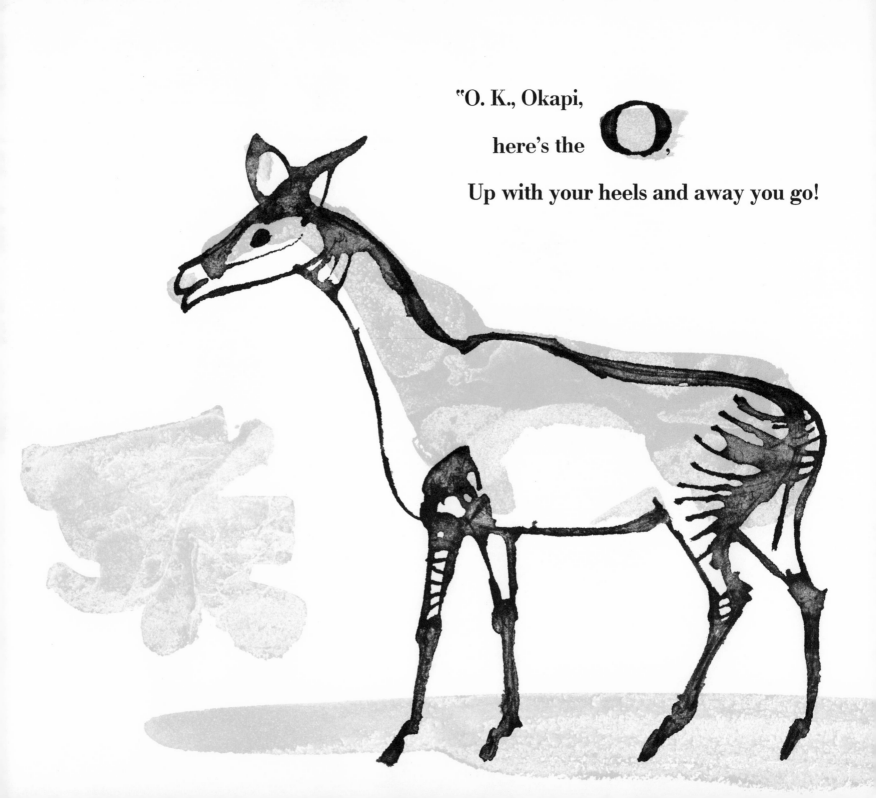

"O. K., Okapi,

here's the O,

Up with your heels and away you go!

"Perky potto, silly clown,

Shall have the **P**, if he'll come down.

"Zig-a-zagga runs the Quagga,

And his tail goes wig-a-wagga."

"Ook," said the rook,

"I can't cook.

So give me the  **R** before it's took."

"Horrors, Sculpin, you look fierce;

You'll never make it with S. S. Pierce.*

* AUTHOR'S NOTE: I know, I know: it's S. S. Pierce,**
                 Which only makes the Sculpin worse.
** EDITOR'S NOTE: Suppliers of fine foods, operating
                  from Boston, reputed to have made
                  their start in the Garden of Eden.

"Tumblebug, you take the **T**.

Just six to go, and I'll be free!

"Umm," said Adam,

"Who are you?

The 'umming bird?

So take the U.

"Viper, viper,  **V** for you.

Up the chimney; down the flue!

"Waddle, waddle, wombat,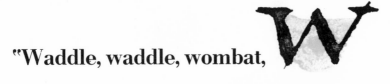

Is just the letter meant for you.

is the unknown quantity

Which I can't name and you can't see."

"Why, oh Y," the ak said sadly,

"Am I always snarled so badly?"

"**Z** for you, zebu. You're looking thinner.

I wonder what Eve has fixed for dinner."

So off he went, with a wave to the critters,

Dreaming of apple pie and fritters

Of applesauce and apple coupe,

But what he got was

ALPHABET SOUP